Play ● Learn

Sticker Activity Fun
Busy Bugs

priddy ● books
big ideas for little people

Picture problem

Which jigsaw piece completes the picture?

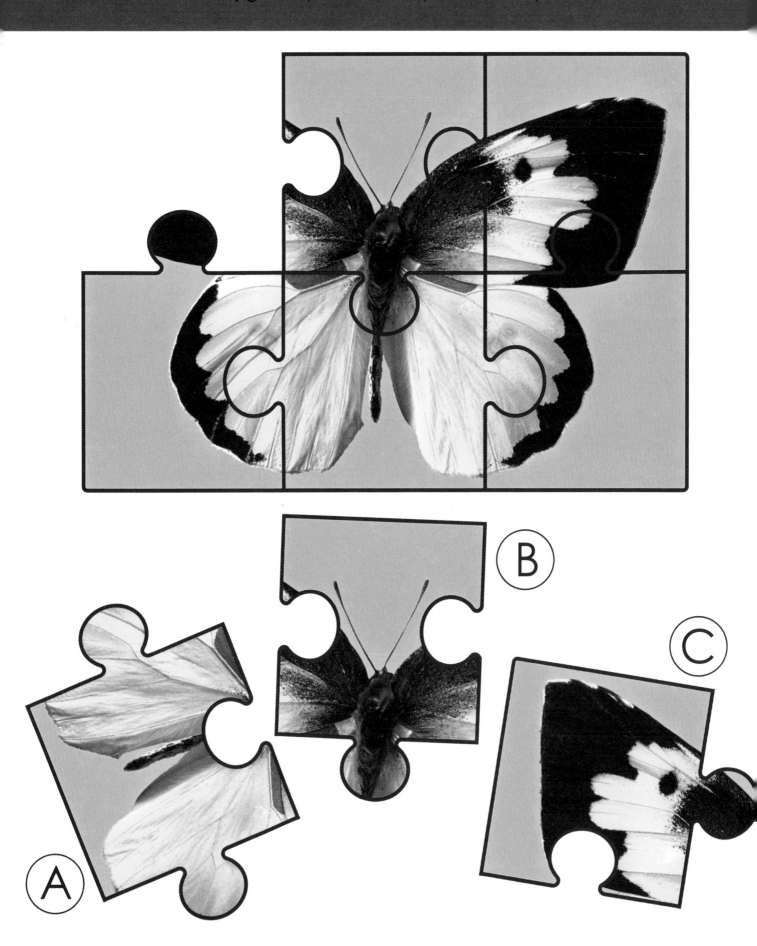

Follow the lines

Use your pen to trace over the lines between the bugs.

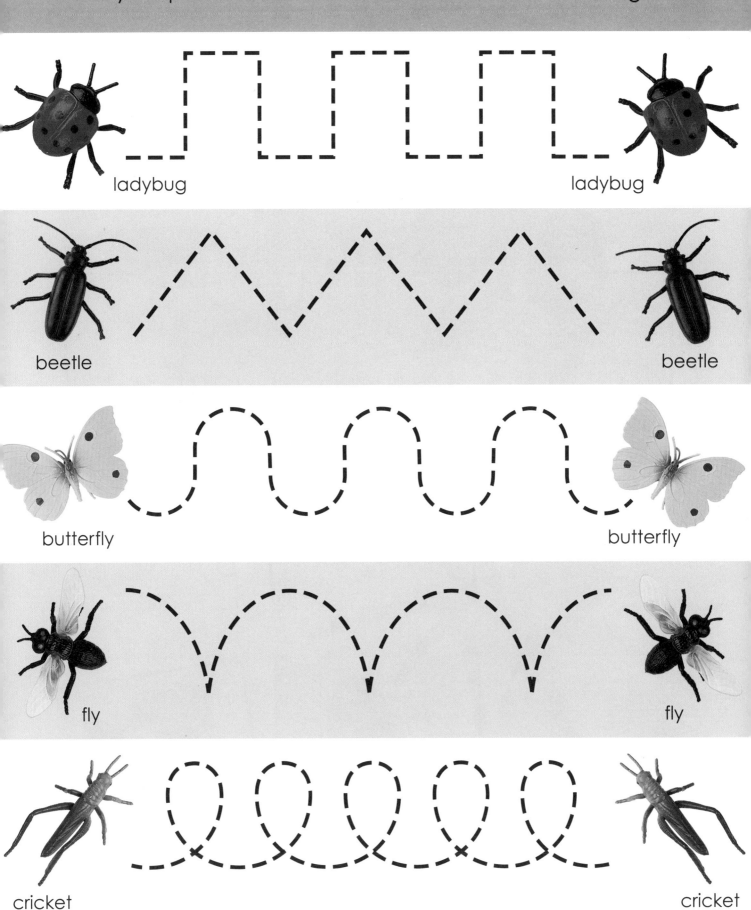

ladybug ladybug

beetle beetle

butterfly butterfly

fly fly

cricket cricket

Counting bugs

Count the bugs and little critters and write the numbers of each in the boxes.

How many praying mantids can you count?

How many snails can you count?

How many
butterflies can
you count?

How many
ladybugs can
you count?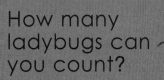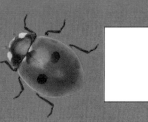

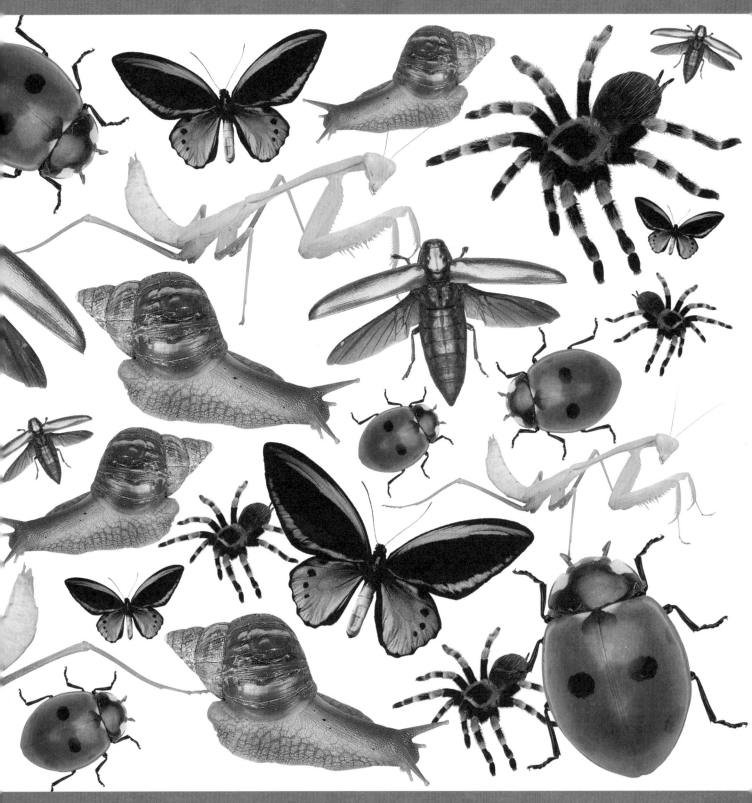

How many
beetles can
you count?

How many
spiders can
you count?

Bug pictures

Find the bug stickers, then color in the pictures.

dragonfly

beetle

Drawing bugs

Look at the picture and word, then trace the outlines.

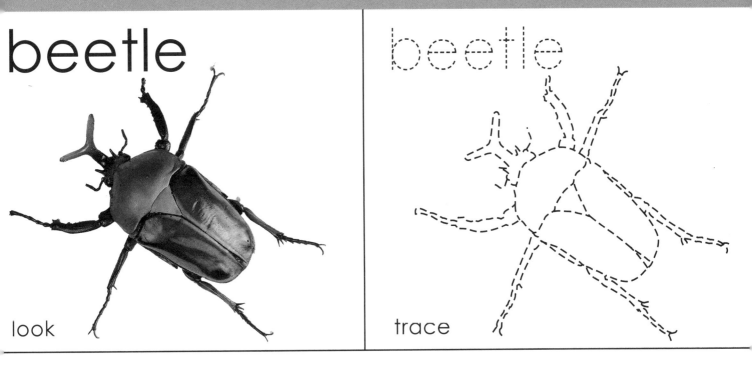

beetle

look

beetle

trace

Now draw the beetle and write the word.

b _ _ _ _ _

Matching letters

Draw a line between each creature and the letter
its name begins with.

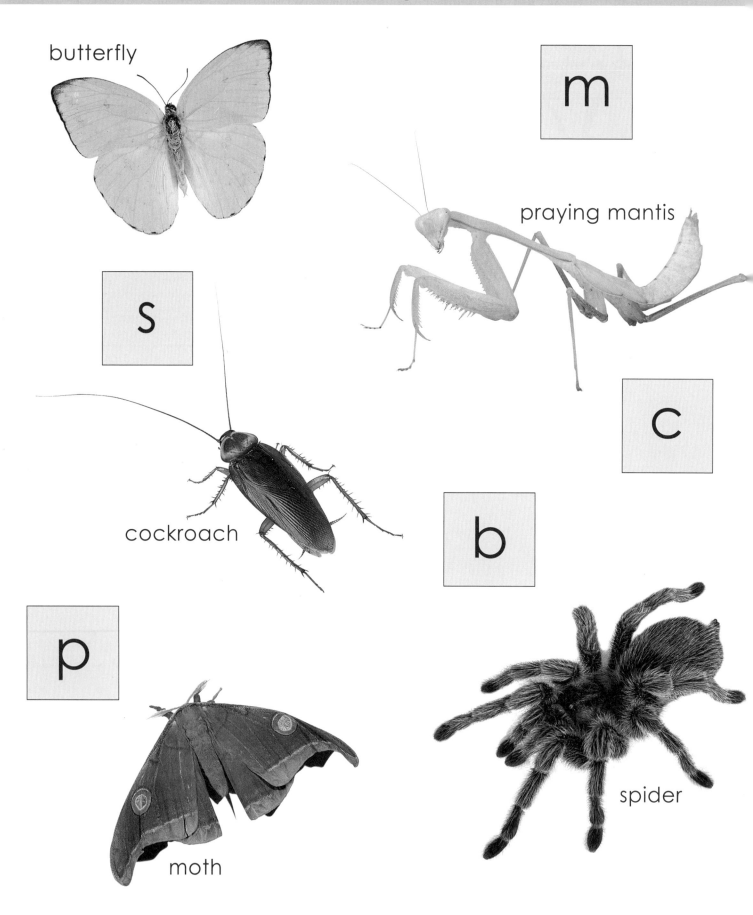

butterfly

m

praying mantis

s

c

cockroach

b

p

moth

spider

Adding bugs

Write the numbers of bugs in the boxes, then add them together.

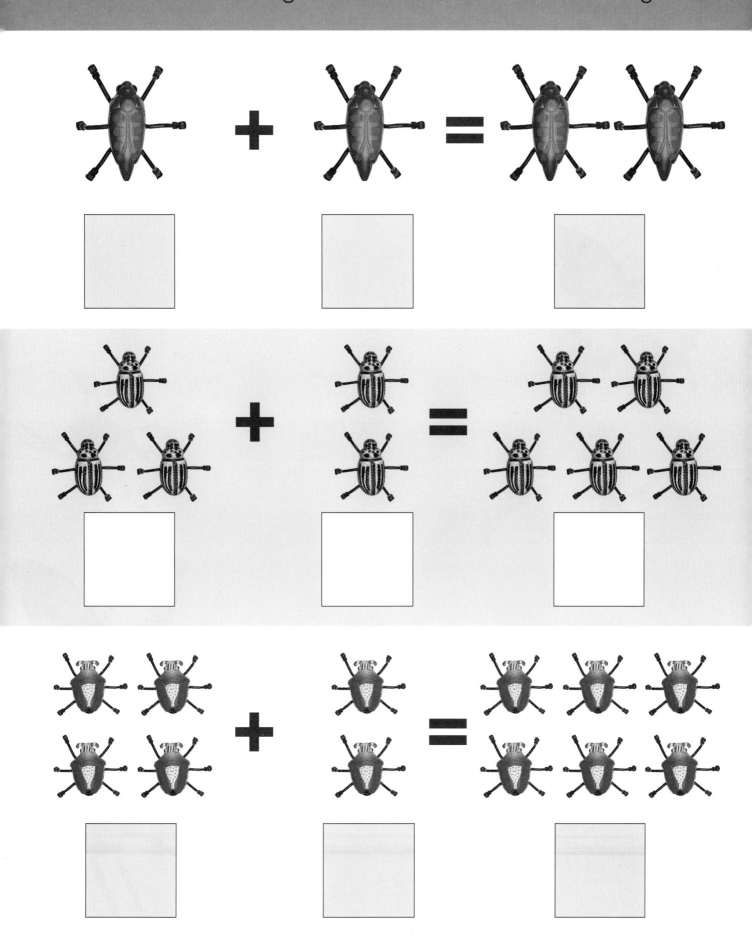

Mix and match

Draw lines between the matching pairs of creatures.

3

4

Who's missing?

Which of the bugs in picture A is missing from picture B?

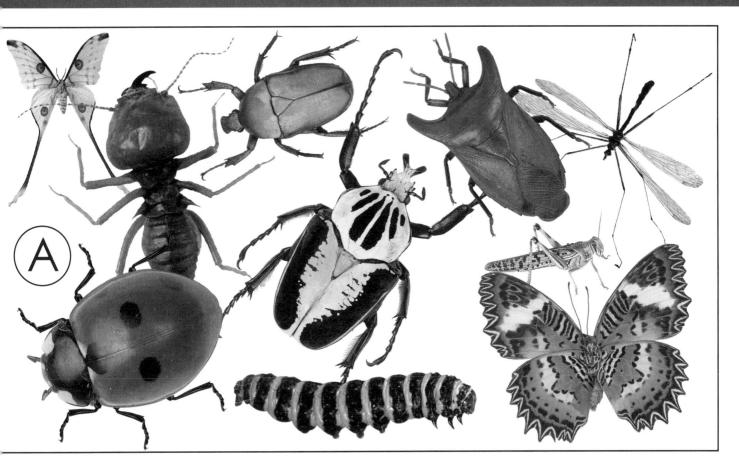

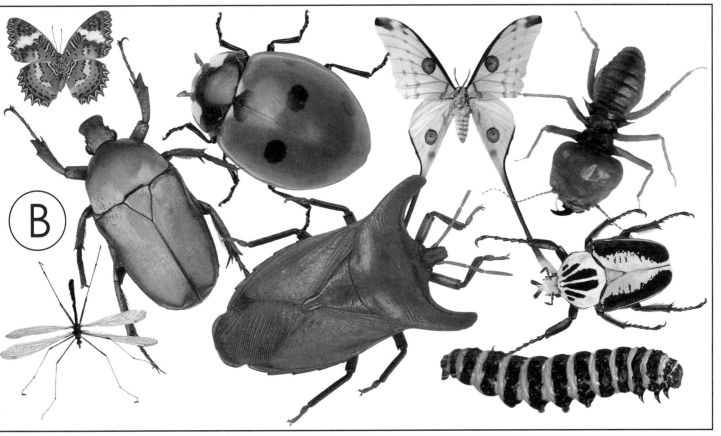

butterfly

butterfly

look

trace

Now draw the butterfly and write the word.

b_____

How many?

Count the bugs and write each number in the boxes.

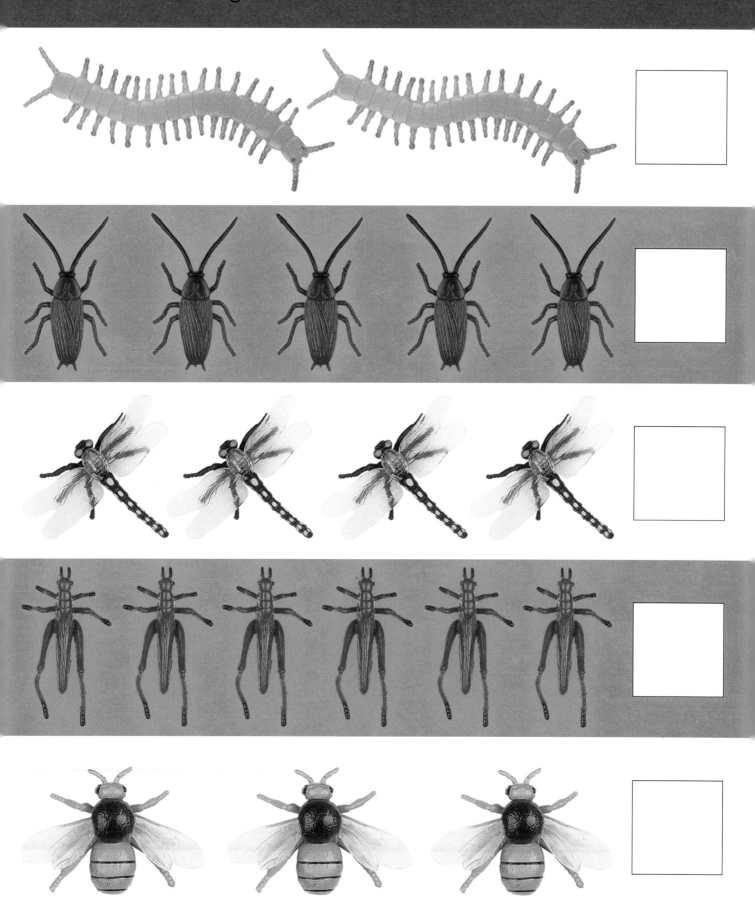

Find the stickers

Find the butterfly stickers that fit the spaces below.
Which one matches the picture?

Dot to dot

Join the dots to complete the bug pictures, then color them in using the colored dots as a guide.

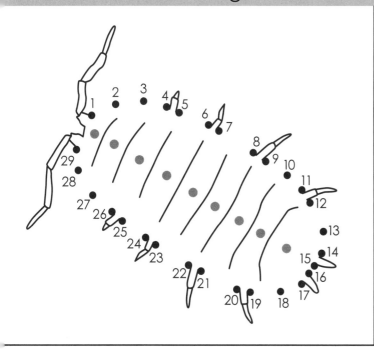

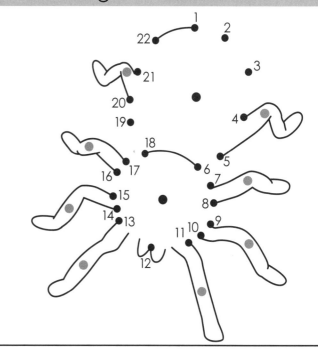

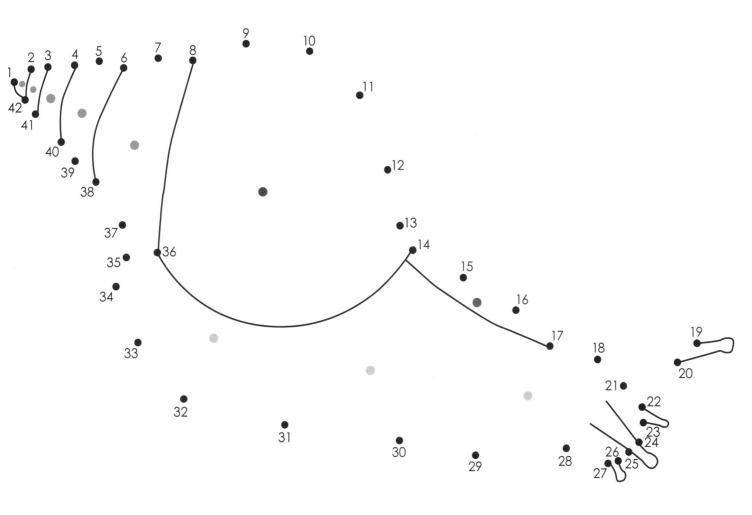

What's different?

There are six differences between these two pictures.
Circle each difference on picture B when you spot them.

Sunflower maze

Find a way through the maze that takes the bee to the sunflower.

start

finish

Butterfly count

Write the number of each color of butterfly in the boxes.

How many
white butterflies
can you count?

How many
yellow butterflies
can you count?

How many
green butterflies
can you count?

How many
orange butterflies
can you count?

How many
purple butterflies
can you count?

How many
blue butterflies
can you count?

Drawing spiders

Look at the picture and word, then trace the outlines.

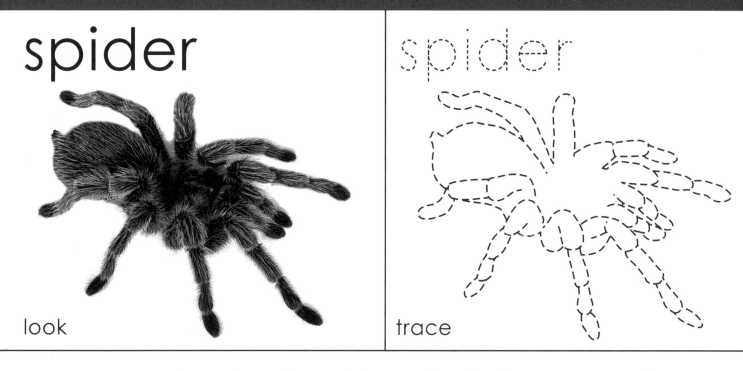

spider

look

spider

trace

Now draw the spider and write its name.

s_ _ _ _ _

moth

beetle

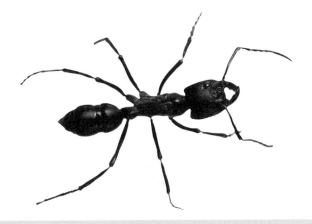

ant

butterfly

What's different?

There are six differences between these two pictures.
Circle the differences on picture B when you find them.

A

B

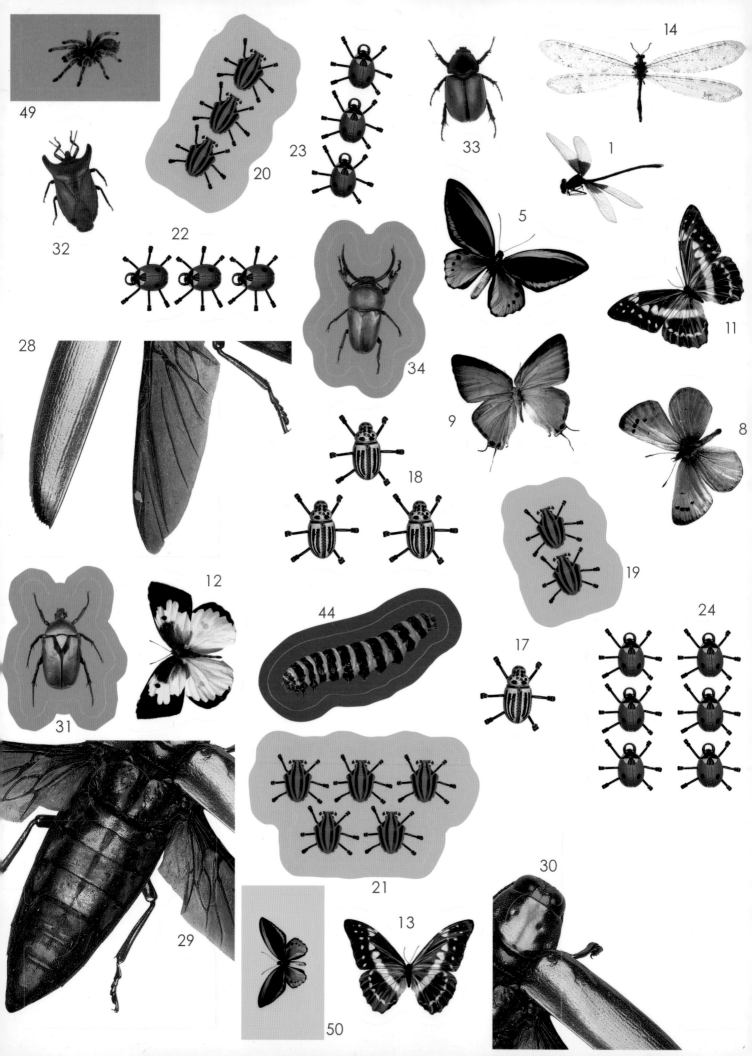

49

20

23

33

14

1

32

22

5

11

28

34

9

8

18

12

31

44

19

24

17

30

29

50

13

21

51

35

45

48

6

39

16

27

26

40

4

2

42

36

15

7

3

38

25

10

41

43

47

37

46

52

Butterfly trail

Which trail takes the small butterfly to the big one?

Scorpion scene

Use your pens or pencils to color in this scorpion picture.

Drawing dragonflies

Look at the picture and the word, then trace the outlines.

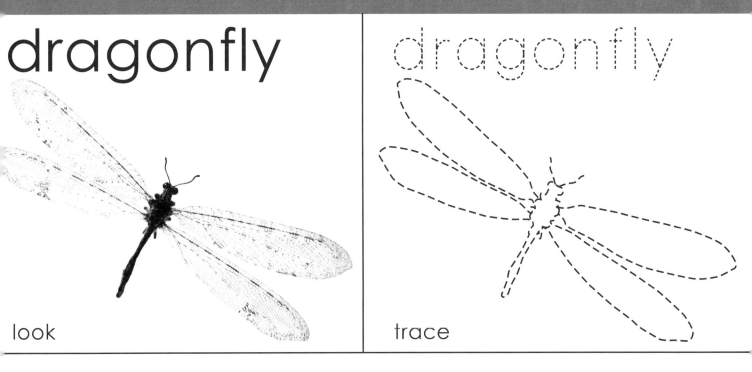

dragonfly

look

dragonfly

trace

Now draw the dragonfly and write its name.

d _ _ _ _ _ _ _ _ _

In the garden

Use your pens or pencils to color in this bug scene.

Writing practice

Trace over the letters of the bug names below.

praying mantis

praying mantis

scorpion

scorpion

spider

spider

caterpillar

caterpillar

Drawing snails

Look at the picture and word, then trace the outlines.

snail

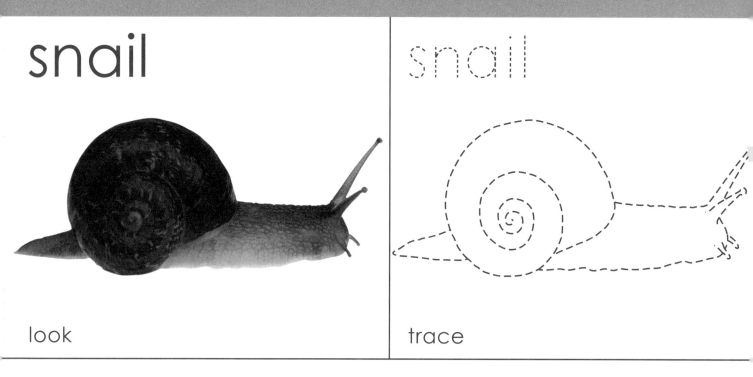

look

snail

trace

Now draw the snail and write its name.

s _ _ _ _ _

Ant maze

Can you find a way through the maze for the
ant to reach the other ants?

start

finish

What's different?

Which one of these creatures is different from the others?

Missing halves

Find the stickers, then draw the other halves of the bugs.

13

butterfly

14

dragonfly

Adding bugs

Find the stickers, write the numbers of bugs in the boxes,
then add them together.

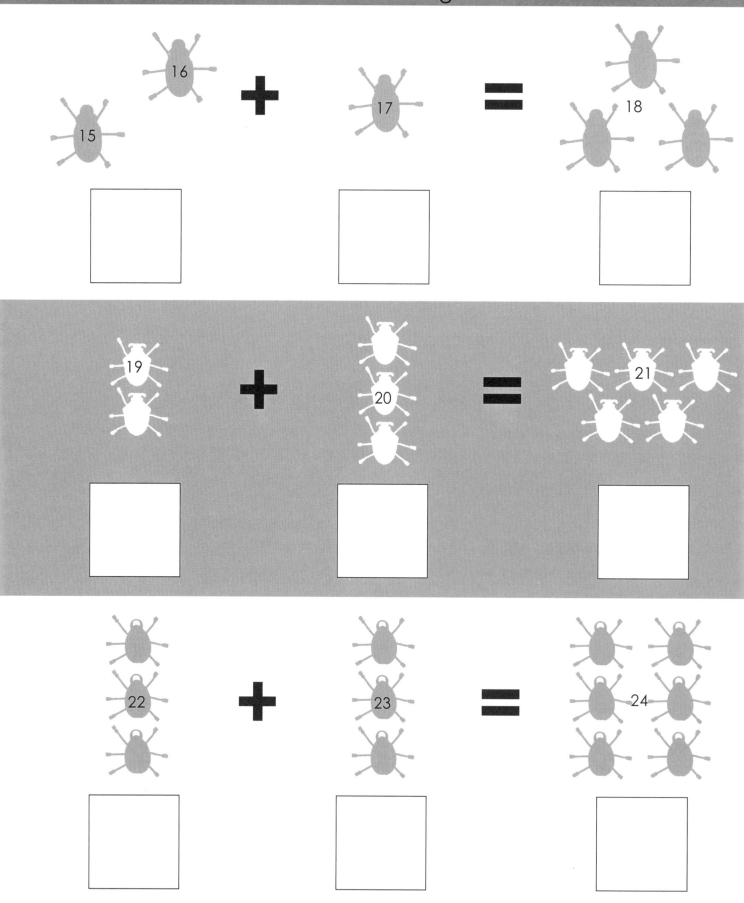

Jigsaw puzzle

Find the jigsaw stickers that complete the pictures below.

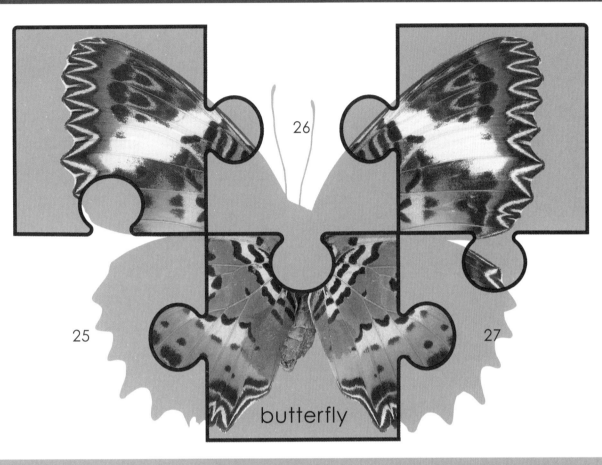

26

25

27

butterfly

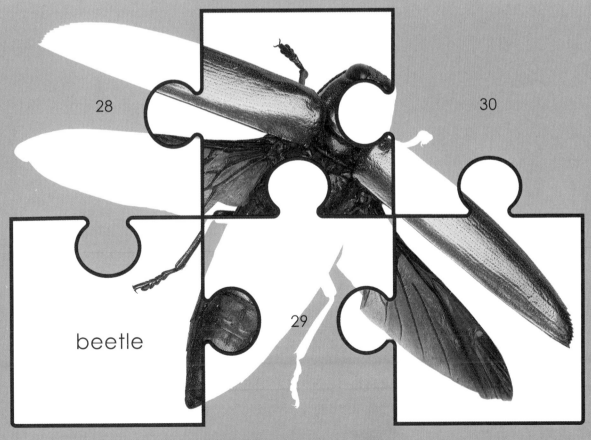

28

30

beetle

29

Bug pictures

Find the stickers, then color in the pictures that match.

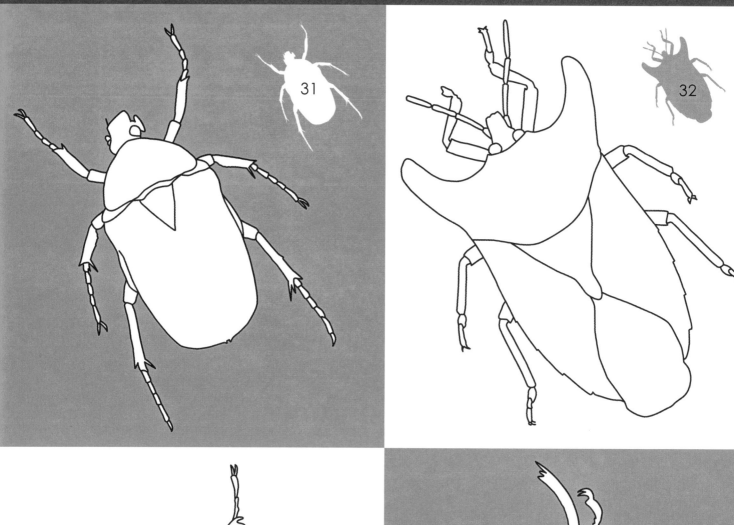

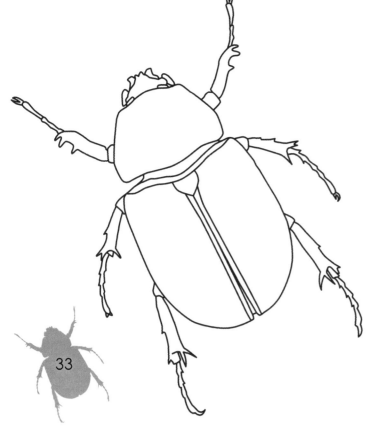

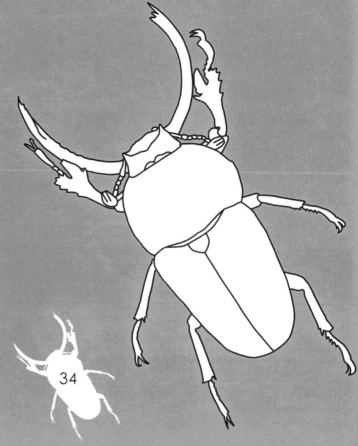

Bug words

Trace over the letters of the bug words below.

wings

tail

horns

legs

Dot to dot

Join the dots to complete these bug pictures, then color them in using the colored dots as a guide.

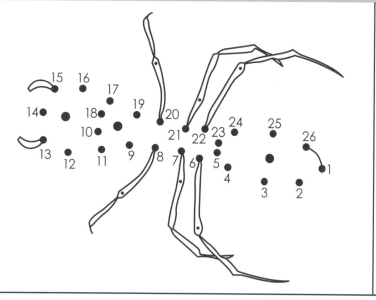

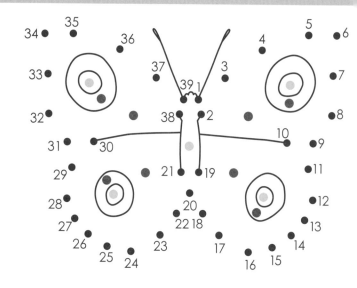

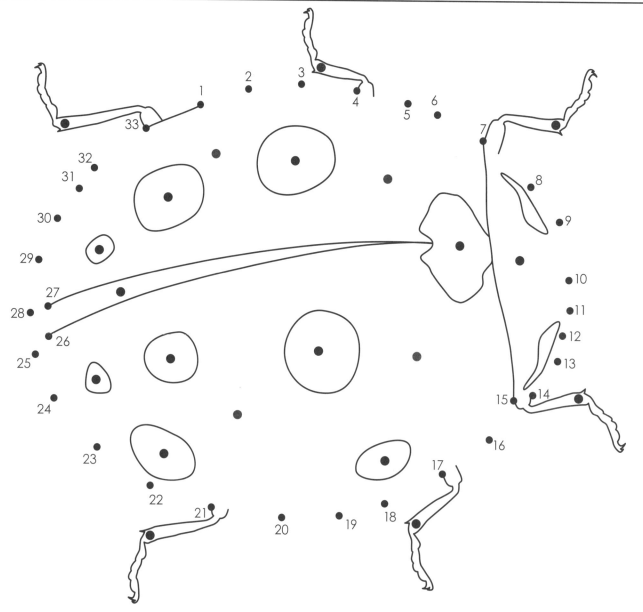

Exactly the same

Only two of these butterflies are exactly the same.
Look closely to find them.

Number practice

Trace the outlines to practice writing numbers and find the stickers that fit on the opposite page.

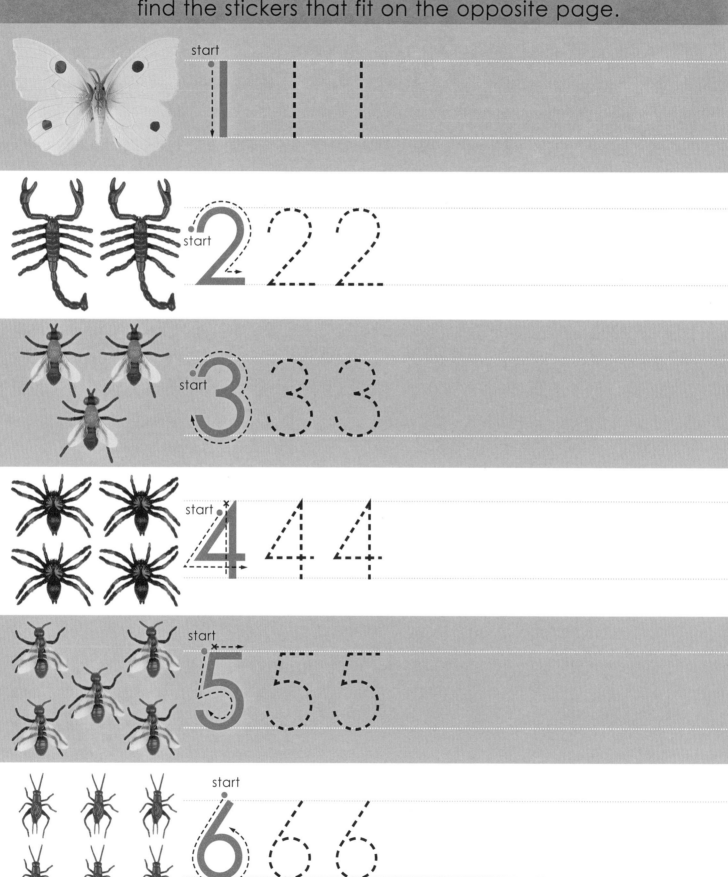

start
1 1 1

start
2 2 2

start
3 3 3

start
4 4 4

start
5 5 5

start
6 6 6

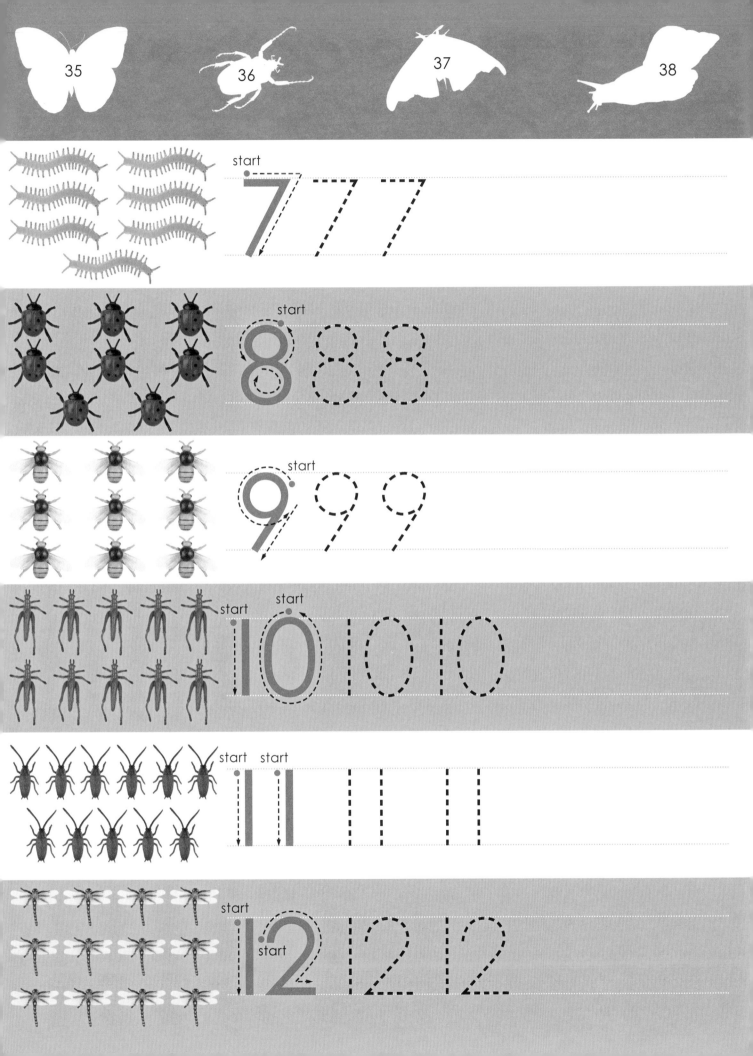

35   36   37   38

start
7 7 7

start
8 8 8

start
9 9 9

start start
10 10 10

start start
11 11 11

start
start
12 12 12

Letter practice

Trace the outlines to practice writing letters and find the stickers that fit on the opposite page.

start
 A

start
 a

start
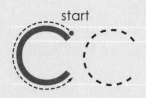 B

start
 b

start
 C

start
 c

start
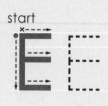 D

start
 d

start
 E

start
 e

start
 F

start
f

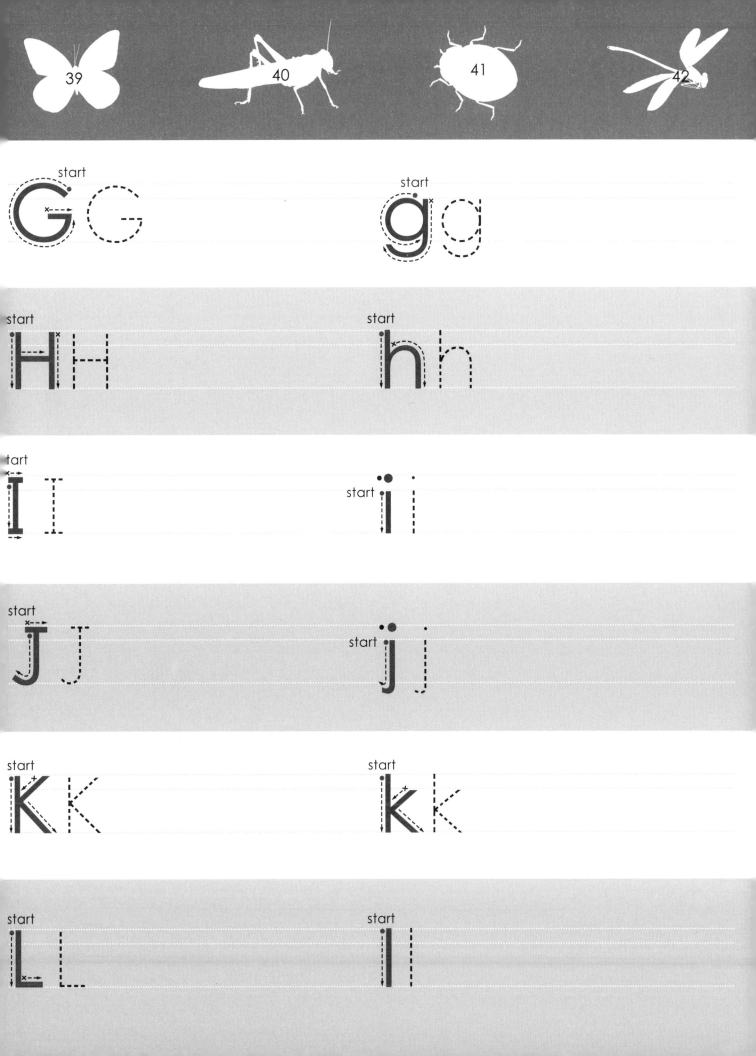

39

40

41

42

start
G G

start
g g

start
H H

start
h h

tart
I I

start
i i

start
J J

start
j j

start
K K

start
k k

start
L L

start
l l

Letter practice

Trace the outlines to practice writing letters and find the stickers that fit on the opposite page.

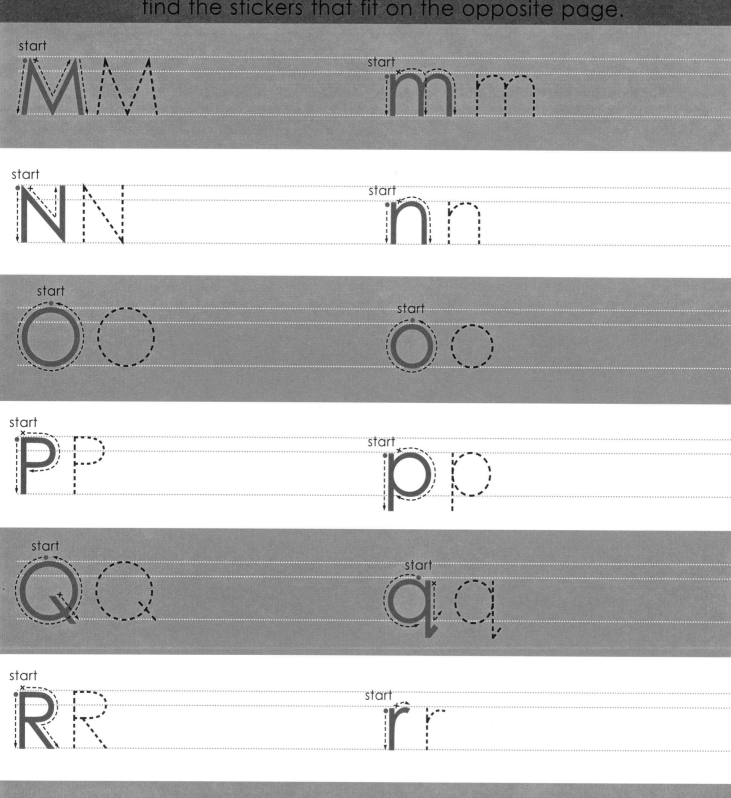

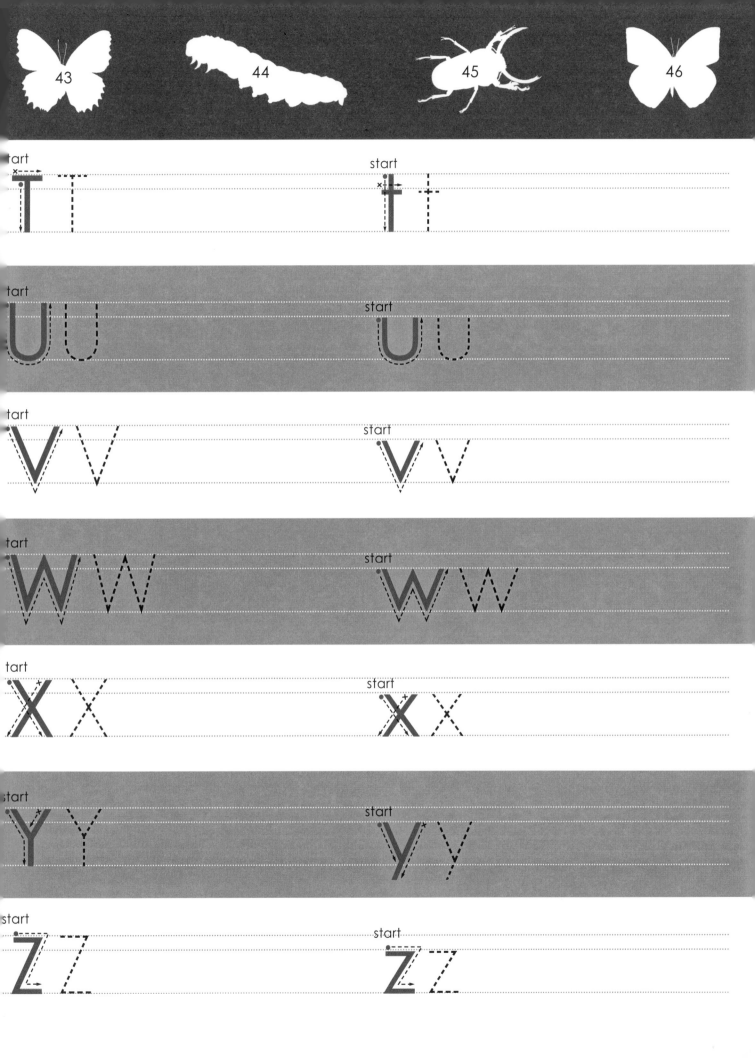

43 44 45 46

start
Tt

start
Tt

start
Uu

start
Uu

start
Vv

start
Vv

start
Ww

start
Ww

start
Xx

start
Xx

start
Yy

start
Yy

start
Zz

start
Zz

Word search

Find the stickers, then look for the words in the box.

b	u	t	t	e	r	f	l	y	e
a	y	s	a	a	m	k	t	a	a
r	e	x	n	e	i	d	r	n	r
e	h	e	t	a	o	r	z	c	w
s	w	o	i	o	i	x	l	c	i
p	i	u	m	t	e	l	i	o	g
i	y	l	s	r	e	m	t	u	b
d	a	e	x	r	m	h	o	r	r
e	q	e	t	h	u	e	n	t	m
r	c	z	s	l	i	s	a	m	h

 snail

 earwig

 spider

 butterfly

 ant

 moth